PENGUIN WORKSHOP
An imprint of Penguin Random House LLC, New York

First published in the United States of America by Penguin Workshop,
an imprint of Penguin Random House LLC, New York, 2020

This paperback edition published by Penguin Workshop,
an imprint of Penguin Random House LLC, New York, 2022

Text copyright © 2020 by Brian McCann
Illustrations copyright © 2020 by Meghan Lands

Visit us online at penguinrandomhouse.com.

Library of Congress Control Number: 2019038777

Manufactured in China

ISBN 9781524793043   10 9 8 7 6 5 4 3 2 1 HH

BY BRIAN MCCANN
ILLUSTRATED BY MEGHAN LANDS

Penguin Workshop

FOR MADELEINE, GLEASON,
AND RUTH—BM

FOR MY MOM, LOVE MEGHAN—ML

TABLE OF CONTENTS

THE INTRODUCTION TO THE BOOK YOU ARE READING

(IT'S SUPPOSED TO SET UP THE STORY. I HOPE IT WORKS!)

Have you ever wondered
what animals think?
Do they ever get bored?
Do they mind that they stink?

Do they look to the sky?
Do they stare at the stars?
Do they know that we're sending
spaceships to Mars?

Do they ever feel jealous?
Or happy? Or sad?
Do they ever think fondly
of a meal they just had?

The answers to these questions are:
you must have, yes, no, yes, yes, no,
yes, yes, yes, and yes.

Hey! That didn't rhyme!
What's the deal with this book?!
Is it filled with good stories
or just gobbledygook?

Well, gobbledygook
is a very good thing.
You might be surprised
at the joy it can bring.

But these are good stories,
epic and true,
although when I say that they're true,
I'm lying to you.

But you'll enjoy them, I promise.
Grab a hot chocolate to drink
'cause it's time to discover
what animals think.

Now, at this point you're probably wondering how I know what animals think. Am I a mind reader? Was I raised by wolves? Did an evil doctor implant a microchip in my brain that allows me to have telepathic communications with our four-legged friends? Those are all great theories, but none are correct. The truth is, I don't know for sure what animals are thinking. I'm just a human being, and human beings don't have superpowers. But I'm a very good judge of character, and when it comes to the stories in this book, I'm pretty sure I'm right about what the animals were thinking. So, let me continue . . .

There's a farm in the country,
a sweet little place,
where life moves along
at a leisurely pace.

It's not far from the city,
the traffic, and crowds,
but instead of bright lights,
it has puffy white clouds.

It goes by the name of
Wannabe Farms.
It's quiet and quaint
with no shortage of charms.

There's a stream, and a lake,
and a big old red barn.
You'll find milk, you'll find eggs,
you'll find large spools of yarn.

For the animals there
life is simple and slow.
They eat and they sleep,
they watch the grass grow.

But the world all around them
is building and growing,
and this gets them thinking,
and ideas start flowing.

They start to have wishes.
They hatch plots and schemes.
They start to think bigger.
They start to have dreams.

But on Wannabe Farms,
dreams never come true,
at least not the way
dreams usually do.

Is that bad? Is that sad?
No, it's not, not at all.
Pursuing a dream
is the point of it all.

So, hold tight the book
at the end of your arms,
and I'll tell you what happened
on . . .

WANNABE FARMS.

THE DAY THE COWS BUILT A CAR FOR THEMSELVES

(iT DiDN'T 80 WELL!)

Our very first story
is about the cows
and how they wanted
to change their lives somehow . . .

You see, the cows spent their days
in a field eating hay,
watching humans drive cars
heading this and that way.

Cars zooming past
was a sight that was new
as the suburbs kept growing
and the new highway came through.

To the cows it looked fun,
driving here, driving there,
heading out on adventures,
the wind in their hair.

They found their field boring,
the same thing every day.
Not much to look at
while chewing dry hay.

If they had a car,
they could go into town,
try lots of new food,
have a good look around.

The cows had an idea:
build a car of their own.
Take it on rides
away from their home.

It was an awful idea.
Cows can't build cars.
It doesn't matter
how determined they are.

They don't understand engines,
computers, or gas.
They don't understand wheels
or windows of glass.

Cows can't hold a hammer.
They can't draw or design.
They can't steer or use blinkers
or read a stop sign.

Cows are wonderful,
gentle, and kind.
But building a car?
Were they out of their minds?

Just for the record, yes, these cows *were* out of their minds. Do you know how much the average cow weighs? Around two thousand pounds! And I'm going to assume that a cow would want to drive around with a friend or two, so that's, like, six thousand pounds, which is the weight of about forty-five people. The cows would need to build a huge truck to achieve their dreams, and I don't need to tell you that cows shouldn't build trucks, either!

When it comes to car building,
cows haven't a clue.
They simply can't understand
the things that *we* do.
Where would they sit?
How fast would they go?

Could they pump their own gas?
The answer is no!
Oh, cows should never,
ever build cars.
But they tried to that day.
They reached for the stars.

They started collecting
what they thought they could use:
a large wooden crate,
a pair of old shoes.

They knew wheels were important
to roll on the ground,
but they didn't know wheels
had to be round.

So they got boxes, a funnel,
an old flowerpot.
Would these work as wheels?
You and I *know* they would not.

How to assemble
the parts they were using?
A cow can't use nails.
That's far too confusing.
A cow can't use tape.
A cow can't use glue.
And cows can't fathom
a screwdriver and screw.
So they shoved things together,
tied them tight with a hose.
How the cows thought of that
nobody knows.

Well, it took them all day,
but at last they were done.
One cow stood in the car
and . . . it didn't run.

How odd, how strange,
the car didn't go.
This wasn't much fun.
It couldn't even go slow.

Then they noticed an apple
fall off of a tree.
As it rolled down the hill,
it gathered up speed!

They looked at each other,
then looked to the hill.
Then they all started pushing.
They wanted a thrill!
To the top, to the top,
they hauled their contraption,
eagerly wanting
some sweet downhill action.

They got their cow car
up next to the tree.
Then they *all* got in
and counted—One! Two! Three!
Then—*crash*! It collapsed!
It smashed to the ground.
Those cows were so heavy.
It was such a loud sound!

They all tumbled out.
The tree was still shaking.
And that was the end
of the car they were making.

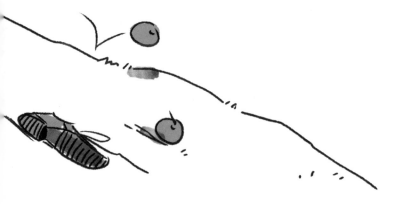

But as the branches kept swaying,
apples fell off the tree,
filling the car
with a delicacy!
Delicious, nutritious,
what a wonderful treat.
There were more than enough
tasty apples to eat.

And as the cows looked around,
what did they see?
All sorts of fresh food
growing for free!
Alfalfa and clover,
corn and small flowers,
endless green grasses,
they could be eating for hours!

They celebrated and danced.
They all let out a moo!
And that was when
they noticed the view!
From high on the hill
they could see the whole town.
They could see every town
for miles around.
What a view! What a sight!
What a wonderful thrill!
The cows' dreams had come true
on the top of that hill.

No car was needed,
no roads and no driving,
to see far-off cities
and feel they were thriving.

They couldn't believe it.
They hadn't a care,
surrounded by food,
the wind in their hair!

What an adventure.
What a success.
They loved their new home
with the hilltop address!

The view was exciting.
The food wasn't boring.
They were giddy and happy.
Their spirits were soaring.

And this wouldn't have happened
if they didn't try.
If they were content
watching cars driving by.

29

But on that fateful day,
they decided to see,
if they tried their hardest,
how good life could be.

Do you have a dream
that you want to come true?
Well, before you pursue it,
here's a message for you:

There's no better time
to get going than now,
unless you're planning
to build a car for a cow!

Don't pursue that dream. It's a real bad idea. I think
I've made that abundantly clear in this story. It would
be really dangerous, and you wouldn't make any money
because cows don't have money to buy cars.

Thank you.

THE DAY THE CHICKENS TRIED TO BUILD A FLAT-SCREEN TV

(SPOILER: IT WENT POORLY.)

When the cows spent a day
constructing their car,
the chickens were watching it all
from afar.

They heard all the mooing,
they saw all the fun,
then they witnessed
the massive destruction.

Pursuing a dream
looked like a fun thing to do.
It didn't matter at all
if it only sort of came true.

But when chickens have dreams,
you better take cover.
Those birds go bananas.
They all act like each other!

They get so excited.
They form a huge flock.
Their eyes get gigantic.
They cluck and they squawk.

They're nervous by nature.
They herk and they jerk!
This jittery crew
goes completely berserk!

Yes, when chickens have dreams,
you should stay far away.
Let me tell you a story
that happened one day . . .

It seemed like a day
that was just like the rest.
The chickens were quiet,
spending time on their nests.

But as evening arrived
with nothing to do,
the chickens got bored,
the chickens felt blue.

Wasn't there something
they could do as a group?
Some way to have fun
right there in the coop?

Then the farmer did something
that excited them all.
He quickly installed
a magic box on his wall.

The box had arrived
that day on a truck.
And when it lit up,
they all let out a cluck!

They stared for a second,
mesmerized by the glow,
then flocked in an instant
to the farmer's window.

Pushing and shoving,
they wanted to see.
What was this thing?
(It's called a TV.)

But its name didn't matter,
not important at all.
The chickens just wanted
this thing on the wall.

A mystical box
playing wonderful things.
They cock-a-doodled and dooed!
And flapped their short wings!

Every channel he changed to,
every image they saw,
sent them into a frenzy,
filled them with awe!

Boxing, bobsledding,
discount bedding,
a commercial for cars,
a royal wedding,

a cat on a wire,
a roaring campfire,
a children's choir,
a washer and dryer!
Dolphins, soccer,
magic, and cakes.
Women in trucks,
men using rakes.

Movies and sports,
fun videos,
plays and cartoons,
all kinds of weird shows!
A girl singing a song,
two men dancing along,
a woman in a sarong,
a monk hitting a gong!

The TV was amazing!
They must get one, but how?
Then they quickly decided
they would build one right now!

But before we go on,
let's take a moment or two,
and discuss if building TVs
is something chickens should do . . .

To them it seemed simple
to build a TV,
but that idea is absurd
for a chicken, you see.

Not that I'm saying
chickens aren't smart.

But are they as smart as an electrical engineer who understands pixels, gases, and other electrically neutral, highly ionized substances? Are they as smart as Donald Bitzer, Gene Slottow, and Robert Wilson, who in 1964 invented the first plasma display panel that led to the flat-screen TV? Are they as smart as Philo T. Farnsworth, who in 1927 invented what is known as an all-electronic image pickup device, which then became the first television ever?

No. Chickens aren't.

They don't understand airwaves, computers, or cable.
And building large screens?
Chickens simply aren't able!

TVs beam and they stream.
They're controlled by remote.
They're high-end electronics
using currents and volts.

They have plugs, they have channels,
aluminum frames.
They can store your old photos.
They play video games.

TVs are amazing,
wonderful things.
And they can't be constructed
by things that have wings!

But this crazed flock of chickens
had TV on the brain,
so they tried to construct one,
and it was completely insane.

They ran in every direction!
Hitting trees and each other!
One ran over his cousin!
One slammed into his mother!

Two hens knocked over
a big bottle of glue,
getting stuck to each other
and an old gym shoe!

They were looking for things
that they thought they would need,
grabbing this, grabbing that,
grabbing it all with great speed.

Some had pipes, some had bags.
There was one with a plate.
There were six stronger chickens
with an old sewer grate!

They had boxes and cans,
an old basketball.
They were out of control,
running fast with it all.

To the coop they all ran,
every rooster and hen,
smashing into it hard!
All one hundred and ten!

What a disaster!
They hit with such force,
the coop slammed to the ground.
It was ruined, of course.

It crashed and it tumbled.
What was up was now down.
What was once facing out
was now smashed to the ground.

But when the dust settled,
they stared with delight
at the wreckage before them
in the warm evening light.

Their coop was demolished,
broken and mangled.
All that remained
was one giant rectangle.

It was perched on its side
lit by the sun's glow.
Bright and inviting,
a screen ready to go!

The chickens stared at their shadows.
They were nicely projected
right onto the screen.
It was more than expected.

Then a shadow was seen
of hens stuck to a shoe.
The others let out a cackle
for a minute or two!

They liked what they saw!
More got in on the action!
They loved to perform!
It was pure satisfaction!

Some started to dance.
Some did funny walks.
Some sat and enjoyed.
Some let out loud squawks.

Oh, what a show
on this rectangular panel.
They'd just created
their own chicken channel!

At the end of their days
they'll no longer feel blue.
They'll entertain one another.
They'll have something to do!

We knew that the chickens
couldn't build a TV,
but what they accomplished
was almost better, you see.

They create their own plays.
They create their own shows.
They create their own dances.
They're show business pros!

The rest of their coop
lay all mashed in a heap,
so they'd have to go find
a new place to sleep.

But as long as the sun
gently sets in the west,
their screen would be working.
They'd take care of the rest.

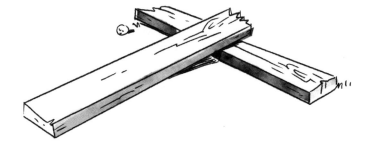

THE DAY THE PIGS TRIED TO LIVE LIKE HUMANS

(GUESS WHAT? IT WAS AN ABSOLUTE CATASTROPHE!)

Out in the country,
on Wannabe Farms,
the gentle beasts in the barnyard
were displaying their charms.

From the cows that attempted
to build a cow car
to the talented chickens
that had become "TV" stars.

Something had happened,
something quite rare.
Something was different.
There was change in the air.

The creatures were dreaming
of things they could do,
of hopes and of wishes,
of things to pursue.

The idea was growing.
It was picking up steam.
Pursuing a dream
was becoming mainstream!

On one summer day,
it happened again,
far away in the field
in a small wooden pen.

The flat-snouted pigs
with their curlicue tails
were eating their slop
out of old rusty pails.

They were snorting and grunting,
making a mess,
when two stepped aside,
away from the rest.

They started to wonder,
what were they doing?
Just standing in mud,
chomping and chewing.

Is this what life was about?
Doing nothing all day?
Lying around?
Having nothing to say?

Who had decided
this is how pigs should act?
Well, it had never been questioned
as a matter of fact.

But the view from their pigsty
had become a production.
Beyond the farm fields,
towns were under construction.

They saw homes being built
and new schools in view.
The humans lived nicely!
Couldn't pigs, too?

These two pigs believed
pigs could do so much more,
from the sow to the warthog
to the hairy wild boar.

·SOW·

·WARTHOG·

·WILD BOAR·

They thought that all pigs,
the big and the small,
could live the good life
away from their stall.

They thought pigs could be fancy,
witty, and smart.
They thought pigs should have manners
and enjoy works of art.

Pigs had so much potential!
They had so much to share!
Living life in the mud?
Well, it didn't seem fair!

There could be a pig school.
There could be a pig city.
There could be pig elections
and a full pig committee.

This was their moment!
This was their time!
The dawn of a new age!
The dawn of the swine!

The rest of the pigs
thought they were crazy.
Pigs shouldn't be fancy.
Pigs should be lazy.

But the two were convinced,
they so firmly believed,
that a pig renaissance
could be achieved.

So the pig pair set off
on a noble pig quest
to build a grand kingdom
and return for the rest.

It might take them months,
it might take them years,
so they said their goodbyes
with pig hugs and pig tears.

Then they probably walked
just a minute or two
when a grand opportunity
came into view.

In the back of the farmhouse,
just out to the east,
the farmer had set
a delectable feast!

It all was unguarded.
No one was around.
They couldn't believe it!
What good fortune they'd found!

He must be throwing a party.
Lots of folks must be coming.
It was an elegant spread.
The pigs' brains started humming!

If the farmer could dine
at a big fancy table,
couldn't pigs, too?
They were certainly able!

What a wonderful chance
to act civilized!
No more head in a bucket!
No more swatting at flies!

They'd sit on real chairs,
use forks and use knives,
sip drinks from cups,
have the time of their lives!

They'd prove to themselves
that pigs can be classy,
that they don't have to be grimy,
stinky, and gassy.

They'd cross their legs and laugh loudly,
eat creams and munch cakes,
have bowls of spaghetti,
drink sweet chocolate shakes.

So one pulled out a chair
for the other to sit.
He nodded his thanks
and climbed onto it.

He tried to sit upright
like he'd seen people do,
but pigs can't sit upright.
That statement's just true!

His legs stuck straight out.
His arms waved in the air.
He wiggled and squirmed
in the uncomfortable chair.

He couldn't get close
to the toast or the jelly,
because blocking the way
was his large piggish belly.

He reached for a drink,
letting out a soft snort,
but he just couldn't reach it.
His arms were too short.

But they didn't give up.
They would not be deterred.
Pigs can be stubborn
as you've probably heard.

They circled the table,
staring up at the treats,
at the stacks of warm pies
and at the goodies and sweets.

But how could they get them?
What could they do?
Let's stop for a second
and think this one through . . .

Okay, if two pigs leave on a journey to create a new
pig kingdom and suddenly find themselves looking at
a big fancy table covered with snacks, and they want
to eat the snacks, well, they don't really have
many options.

We know they can't sit on the chairs—
because they are pigs.

We know they can't drive a truck over to the table
and scrape off all of the food with a magic
food-scraping shovel—because they are pigs.

In fact, we know they can really do only one thing:
ACT LIKE PIGS!—because they are pigs.

And that's what they did.

When an animal's hungry,
when it wants to get food,
it can forget to act kindly.
It can start to act rude.

It's not the animal's fault.
It's known as instinct.
They become unpredictable.
They no longer think.

And that's just what happened.
They got upset and riled.
They got panicked and kooky.
The pigs went hog wild.

It was mayhem and madness.
They were oinking and squealing.
They were running in circles.
They were rocking and reeling.

Now, you probably think
that pigs can't move quickly
with short little legs
and bodies built thickly.

But these pigs were fast.
They wanted *on*to that table.
They kept building up speed
and were finally able!

One jumped on a bench.
The other jumped on a chair.
Then they both took a leap
and went high in the air.

They slammed onto the feast,
exhausted and sweaty.
Cakes and candies went flying,
so did the spaghetti.

It was total destruction.
The pigs rolled in potatoes.
They gorged on a sandwich
and danced in tomatoes.

Then they looked at themselves
all covered in food,
and suddenly both pigs
were in a very good mood!

They didn't look filthy,
smelly, or messy.
They looked kind of fancy,
classy, and dressy.

A cake for a hat.
Spaghetti for hair.
The most civilized pigs
you would find anywhere!

Salad for pants.
Red stains for shoes.
A shirt made of pudding.
Lollipops for tattoos.

They were expressing themselves—
very unique.
Pig works of art—
trendy and chic!

They sauntered right back
to where the other pigs lay
and showed off their new look.
It was a historical day.

The other pigs stared,
becoming inspired,
and the old way of the pig
was quickly retired.

All the pigs wanted
cake hats, too!
Being pigs with pizzazz
was exciting and new!

They shot off to the table.
They rolled in the mess,
making string bean tuxedoes
and a Cobb-salad dress.

It was a massive pig party,
a real pig celebration.
The best day of their lives.
They were filled with elation.

This was the feeling
the pigs had desired.
They were living life better.
They were living inspired.

To be fancy like humans?
They couldn't compete!
But to be fancy pigs
they just wear what they eat!

THE DAY THE SHEEP WANTED TO BECOME BARBERS

(IT'S LITERALLY IMPOSSIBLE, BY THE WAY, SO IT WAS A HUGE MESS!)

If you're keeping score,
here's what has happened so far:
The cows started it all
by building a car.

That inspired the chickens
to build a TV,
which inspired the pigs
to act all fancy.

So, it happened again,
one day with the sheep,
on a cool, cloudy morning
as the sheep tried to sleep.

Out of the blue
came a construction crew,
stomping right through
the wet morning dew.

They hammered, they hauled,
they hoisted things high.
They were done in an hour,
they did not say goodbye.

It was in the sheep's pasture.
It could not be ignored.
It stood fifty feet tall.
It was a brand-new billboard.

It was huge, it was massive,
it blocked out the sky.
It was something to look at
for the cars that drove by.

The sheep couldn't read it,
but they could certainly see
lots of beautiful models
with their hair wild and free.

The flock soon forgot it,
but four sheep just stared.
There was something about
all that beautiful hair.

Then an Old English sheepdog
came to herd them away.
Off to the shed,
it was sheep-shearing day.

And that's when the thought
jumped into their heads.
They should avoid getting sheared,
cut their own hair instead!

Sheep that get sheared
have no style or grace.
Hair's removed from their bodies.
Hair's removed from their face.

But what if the hair
wasn't sheared off completely,
and instead had some style
and was cut cool and neatly?

The idea was exciting!
They'd make it their duty!
The sheep wanted glamour!
The sheep wanted beauty!

Why should the humans
have all of the fun?
Couldn't the sheep
put their hair in a bun?

Or have mohawks, or crew cuts,
or a sheep pompadour,
or high taper fades,
or long braids to the floor!

So the four ducked away.
They escaped from the line.
Hiding in bushes,
biding their time.

Where the cows and the chickens
had tried to build things,
and the pigs had set out
to see what luxury brings,
the sheep had a mission
that was focused and clear.
They needed the tool.
The tool used to shear!

They'd all seen the farmer
do his shearing before,
shaving them bald,
their hair on the floor.

So they hid out all day
until the man was in bed,
then they made their way over
to his sheep-shearing shed.

It was a two-story structure
made just to shave wool.
The door was unlocked,
so they gave it a pull.

Then they raced to the loft.
They knew just what to do.
It was hair-cutting time
for the lamb, rams, and ewe!

This seems like a very good spot to stop and think about things for a second. First of all, I'm guessing you just learned a couple of new words. Maybe you knew that a *lamb* was a younger sheep, but did you know grown male sheep are called *rams* and females are called *ewes*? And guess what, there's a French word coming up very soon! It's the French word for *butt*, so you'll want to remember it. Now, let's talk about the lamb, rams, and ewe for a second. I've seen a lot of sheep, and I'll be honest with you, not once did I say to myself, "That sheep really looks like it knows how to cut hair." Not once did I say, "I would trust that sheep with a sharp hair-cutting tool." I don't know if you've ever noticed, but sheep don't have things like hands and fingers, which are really important when cutting hair and holding sharp objects. But they believed they could do it, and here's what happened . . .

They found the sheep shears
near the wall, on a stool.
They fit in their mouths!
They got covered in drool!

One swung his head wildly
to start cutting hair.
But the blade just got stuck
near a ram's derriere!
(That's the French word that means butt!)

He shot up in pain,
crashing hard on the rail,
landing first on his head,
then smashing down on his tail.

This was all very lucky
simply because
when the shears fell out,
they started to buzz!

The buzz was a sound
the sheep remembered quite clearly,
the sound of a shearing
that happened once yearly.

So they tried it again.
One picked them back up.
He swung his head wildly.
Was it dangerous? Yup.

He clipped easily through
one side of the ewe.
It wasn't pretty, exactly,
and it frightened her, too!

She jumped to the side,
but the loft was so small,
she got buzzed again
when she bounced off the wall!

A big tuft of wool
flew off of her head.
Where there once were cute curls
was a disaster instead!

She wanted to run,
but there was no place to go
while the crazy sheep barber
jerked his head to and fro!

It was total confusion!
Flying wool everywhere.
Now all of the sheep
were losing big clumps of hair.

From all the commotion,
the loft started to bust!
The boards started creaking.
The air filled with dust.

The sheep didn't move.
They were frozen in fear.
Then they looked at each other,
and the carnage was clear.

Their hair looked so awful.
It couldn't look worse!
One looked like a waffle.
One looked like a curse!

They all looked horrendous.
No beauty. No style.
They were mangy and messy.
It had not been worthwhile.

Then one floorboard snapped!
What a frightening sound!
Then the whole loft collapsed!
The sheep fell to the ground!

They landed with force,
and each let out a bleat!
Then they looked at each other . . .
That bleat sounded so neat!

They tried it again,
this sweet one-note song.
One let out a baa!
And the rest joined along.

The sound was enchanting.
The notes swelled in their hearts.
They had created true beauty.
Harmony in four parts!

Despite their bad haircuts,
they were far from upset.
Instead of barbers, they were
a barbershop quartet!

They returned to the pasture,
singing their song.
The flock gathered round,
and all joined along.

It was an odd-looking, sweet-sounding,
magnificent sight,
as their song filled the air
on that beautiful night.

They were patchy, looked silly,
but they just had to grin.
The outside doesn't matter.
Beauty comes from within.

So to sum things up
I just have to say,
if your barber's a sheep,
you should just run away!

THE DAY THE HORSES DECIDED THEY COULD MAKE THE FARM MORE SUCCESSFUL!

(DID YOU GUESS TOTAL DISASTER? YOU'RE RIGHT!)

Wannabe Farms,
where the animals dream,
used to be busy
but was now losing steam.

As you probably know
a new highway came through,
bringing traffic and progress
and that new billboard, too.

It's hard to deny
the strength of these forces,
and they were felt most of all
by the Wannabe horses.

The horses, at one point,
were the stars of the show.
They made Wannabe Farms
a place people would go.

Powerful, pretty
stallions and mares.
Ponies to ride
at the Wannabe Fairs.

There was jumping and polo,
racing and shows.
Trotting and dressage
and horse rodeos.

Crowds came to the farm.
It was *the* place to be.
Business was booming.
It was something to see.

Then slowly but surely
the crowds went away.
No one came to ride.
No one came to play.

The reason was simple.
Out of sight, out of mind.
The people moved on
and left the horses behind.

They lived by the *old* road
that nobody used.
The highway was now
where all the cars cruised.

From that fast-moving freeway
horses couldn't be seen.
Two pastures away
with a lake in between!

And their old horse barn
had lost all its charm.
It could no longer be seen
advertising the farm.

The horses were bitter.
They used to be kings!
They just weren't prepared
for the changes change brings.

Their days were so dull.
They felt trapped by their fences.
They were lonely and bored.
Change has consequences!

They watched as the others
made new dreams come true.
And they began to get jealous.
They didn't know what to do.

How dare they have fun!
How dare they evolve!
The farm was in crisis!
There was a problem to solve!

This farm was for horses!
And the crowds that they bring.
Not for cows building cars
and sheep learning to sing.

Oh, the horses were angry!
Enough was enough!
It was time to do something.
It was time to get tough.

But how to achieve it?
How to get what they needed?
They started kicking and bucking,
and then they stampeded!

They started neighing and snorting.
They were pawing the ground.
It was a loud horse conference
heard for miles around.

Then as quick as it started,
the horse conference stopped,
and up to the barn
all horses clopped.

They stared at the sign,
so big and inviting.
It was clearly important
with its painted-on writing.

Two stories tall.
A beacon to all.
WANNABE FARMS
and a number to call.

The horses all neighed.
They knew just what to do.
They now had a dream,
and they would make it come true.

These horses believed
the barn had to be moved.
And who better to do it
than the powerful hooved.

It must be pushed to the highway,
where it couldn't be missed!
It must block that new billboard!
Oh, they couldn't resist!

Then all of the cars,
all the trucks and the buses,
would see the big barn
and wonder what all the fuss is.

Thousands of people
would see the sign every day!
They'd return to the farm
to ride and to play!

Now . . . this plan of the horses
seemed downright insane.
To move this big barn?
You'd need a freight train.

But then, horses are horses.
They're solid and strong.
They can run two-minute miles
with someone riding along!

But barns aren't just heavy.
This one was immense.
They'd have to push it downhill
and lift it over a fence.

The lake was a problem
they chose to ignore.
They'd figure that out
when they got to the shore.

And this barn was old.
It was a hundred and two!
Was moving it now
a smart thing to do?

No. No it wasn't.
It wasn't smart. Not at all.
This rotted old barn
was destined to fall.

How do I know this? Let me tell you a little
bit about the barn . . .

A hundred and two years ago a group of neighbors all helped a farmer named Obadiah construct his horse stable. They weren't master carpenters by any stretch of the imagination. In fact, most had never built anything before in their lives. So they tried to follow the plans as best they could and, for the most part, did a pretty good job. Truth be told, this barn should have fallen down long ago, but through all of those years, the farm avoided disaster after disaster. Tornadoes narrowly missed it. Heavy rains never challenged it. Nothing ever crashed into it. No fires ever burned it.

This was one of the luckiest barns in the world, and even though its wood was rotting, it still stood proud and tall. Until the day the horses thought it should be moved over to the highway. You really need to be an engineer to successfully move any type of structure, and as smart as horses are, they just aren't trained engineers. They were unable to take into account all the factors and forces that the barn would be subjected to, and because of this, things quickly went haywire.

The horses split into teams,
one in back, one in front.
They started pushing and pulling
and to whinny and grunt.

Support beams were snapping!
The barn started to slide!
Things broke through the walls
that were sitting inside.

A tractor! The stables!
Out came an old truck!
Lots of things were revealed
when that barn came unstuck!

The horses kept pushing,
right through the old fence,
when all of a sudden,
things got very tense!

The barn started moving
all on its own.
There was no one in charge.
Horses were thrown!

Down! Down a hill,
racing fast toward the lake.
It was picking up speed.
An enormous mistake!

It cartwheeled and tumbled.
The sign split in two!
Moving a barn
is something horses can't do!

A door was thrown high!
And as a matter of fact,
all the sides were destroyed,
but the roof was intact!

That roof was so huge,
so heavy and large,
when it smashed into the lake,
it floated out like a barge.

But it didn't float long,
because it hit the far side.
It sort of wobbled a bit,
then its momentum just died.

It didn't sink very much.
The lake wasn't too deep.
And the sound of the crash
brought over the sheep.

The pigs came to look.
The cows came down, too.
And the chickens came over
to see the hullabaloo.

They all stared at the roof
as it sat in the lake.
The horses were silent.
They'd made a mistake.

What had they done?
They had acted so dumb!
And all because
they wanted people to come.

Once bitter and angry
and hungry for fame,
they hung their heads low
and felt a great shame.

They returned to their field
sad and defeated.
Their dream of the crowds
would not be completed.

But down by the lake,
the mood was quite high.
The roof made a bridge
the others could try.

They'd never been able
to cross the small lake.
What the horses had done
was a happy mistake!

It opened a whole new
world to explore.
They'd seen all the horses
but never met them before.

So the cows and the chickens,
the pigs and the sheep,
went to the horse field,
up the hill tall and steep.

They found all the horses
glum and depressed,
and thought this was a problem
that must be addressed.

It was time for a party!
The best party ever!
For the first time in history,
they all were together!

The sheep were the band.
The pigs looked tremendous.
The cows passed out apples.
The Chicken Show was stupendous.

The horses had wanted
new crowds to come,
and by creating a bridge,
what they wanted was done!

They'd no longer be lonely.
The whole farm was connected!
Things worked out much better
than the horses expected!

And you could see the joy
on *every* animal's face.
They knew that some magic
had just taken place.

They were working together
for an evening of fun!
Their five dreams combined
into this stunning new one!

By trying their hardest
they helped one another.
They'd discovered themselves
and discovered each other.

At the end of this night,
all the animals knew,
they'd be there for each other
no matter what they went through.

So they all took a walk
to the now broken sign.
They paid their respects.
They built a small shrine.

Wannabe Farms
had become something new.
A powerful place
where dreams *always* come true.

They'd no longer be bored.
They'd no longer be blue.
To follow their dreams
was all they would do.

That night, all the animals,
every last one,
finally felt happy.
Their lives were now fun.

Or . . .

IT'S THE *EPILOGUE* OF THE BOOK!

(DID i MISS THE WHOLE POINT?)

Perhaps there's no way
to know what animals think.
If they have dreams.
If they enjoy what they drink.

Some people say
they can't think a bit!
That they simply have instincts
and that's simply it!

So, let's take a step back,
give them no credit for thought,
and just look at their actions
and the destruction they brought.

The cows smashed a crate
on the top of a hill,
causing a mess
and a huge apple spill.

The chickens got out
running here, running there,
exploding their coop,
never seeming to care.

The sheep then ruined
the shed used for shearing.
Then they made lots of noise
back in their clearing.

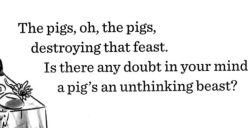

The pigs, oh, the pigs,
destroying that feast.
Is there any doubt in your mind
a pig's an unthinking beast?

The horses, by far,
caused the most harm
by completely destroying
the rest of the farm.

It certainly seems
this is what they would do
if they were left to run wild
for a week or two.

Speaking of which: Who is in charge of the farm? Can you believe that nobody tried to stop any of this from happening? Hello? Farmer? Your farm is becoming a huge mess!

Hello?!

Anyway . . .

Animals are just wild,
some people would say.
They're destructive and rude.
They engage in foul play.

They cannot be trusted.
They get in all sorts of trouble.
And if they're left by themselves,
that trouble will double.

Well . . .

You can look at the damage
and say that it's tragic.
Or you can look at what happened
and *see* there was magic.

Deep in my heart
I know that it's true—
thinking and dreaming
are things all animals do!

But seriously . . . who is in charge
of that farm?

ACKNOWLEDGMENTS

Allow me to thank a few farmhands who made this book possible. First and foremost, the man with the vision and the enthusiasm to turn my silly ponderings into a book, Francesco Sedita! I hope you don't lose your job for taking a chance on me. Then there is my sharp and witty editor, Nathaniel Tabachnik, who took a few stories about some crazy animals and saw the opportunity to explore a whole world. Next there is my incredible art director, Kayla Wasil, who knew right away how Wannabe Farms should look. It was Kayla who introduced me to the insanely talented Meghan Lands! Meghan brought the farm to life and injected so much delightful humor into every drawing. She truly has all the stories jumping off the pages, and I am forever grateful. And to all the incredibly talented and hardworking people at Penguin Workshop, thank you, thank you, thank you!